The Day I Followed the Pickle

CHARACTERS

Jordan

Morgan

Pickle

Esophagus

Stomach

Small Intestine & Large Intestine

SETTING

Jordan's kitchen
Lunchtime, present day

Jordan: Yum, good grilled cheese, isn't it, Morgan?

Morgan: Yeah.

Jordan: Do you ever wonder what happens to food after you eat it?

Morgan: Not really.

Jordan: Well, I do. I think about it a lot. I mean, you eat it, then the rest is a mystery to me.

Morgan: I just eat it.

Pickle: *(whispering)* Hey, Jordan!

Jordan: Who's that? Did you hear something, Morgan?

Morgan: Nope. All I hear is you. And I am trying to read this book.

Pickle: Down here, Jordan! On Morgan's plate.

Jordan: Huh? I only see pickles.

Pickle: That's me! The small one. Pleased to meet you.

Jordan: You're a pickle! And you're talking?

Down here, Jordan!

Pickle: Sure! Morgan can't hear me, so listen up. I heard you wondering about where your food goes after you eat it.

Jordan: Yes, I think about that a lot.

Pickle: Do you want to travel through a digestive system?

Jordan: Travel through one? Sounds weird.

Pickle: I guess it is. But what an adventure, too!

Jordan: I like adventures. OK, let's do it! But how? What do we do first?

Pickle: First, we will shrink you down very tiny so you can climb on my back. Then Morgan will eat us.

Jordan: But won't I get chewed up?

Pickle: You will stay whole. I'll go through all the chewing.

Jordan: Won't Morgan see all this?

Pickle: Are you kidding? Morgan is in another world. He doesn't even notice that you seem to be talking to yourself. Now, repeat after me: *Hickledy, pickledy pack. Put me on Pickle's back.*

Jordan: *Hickledy, pickledy pack. Put me on Pickle's back.* Wow, it worked! And look, Morgan's about to eat us!

Pickle: Hold on!

Morgan: Yum. Pickle.

Pickle: We're in Morgan's mouth. The food gets chewed here. The smaller the pieces, the easier they are to swallow.

Jordan: Morgan's got pretty nice teeth.

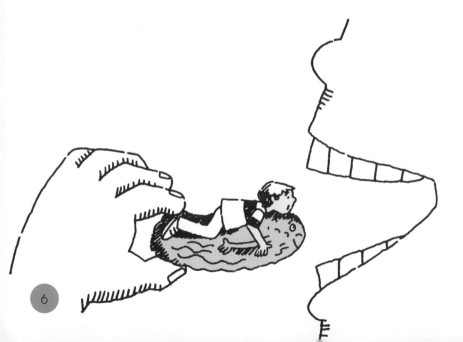

Pickle: And here we go!

Jordan: What's happening?

Pickle: We're heading down the throat. Whee!

Jordan: I feel funny. We're going really fast!

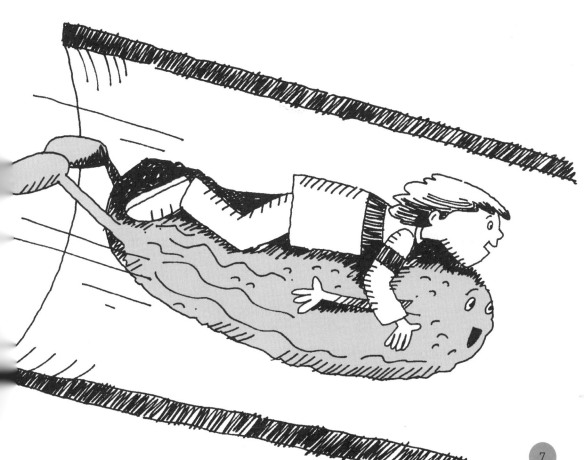

Esophagus: Now for a great big hug!

Jordan: Who are you?

Esophagus: Morgan's esophagus.

Jordan: The esophagus talks, too?

Esophagus: Sure. Come down here and let me give you a hug.

Jordan: Um, I'm not sure I want one.

Esophagus: I'll squeeze you down into the stomach. My muscles will do all the work.

Pickle: It will get a little bumpy. Hold on.

Esophagus: Some people call me a gullet. I'm the tube that goes from the mouth to the stomach. Now squeeze, squeeze.

Pickle: It kind of tickles, huh?

Jordan: I guess.

Esophagus: Well, here you are at the stomach. Enjoy the rest of your trip!

Stomach: Well, hello! Welcome to the stomach. I'll just close up now, so you can't get out yet.

Pickle: Tell us about yourself, Stomach.

Stomach: I'm like a balloon. I can stretch. The more food you eat, the more I'll stretch. Now, time for a great big hug!

Jordan: More hugging?!

Stomach: Yes. I have to break up the food by mashing and stirring it.

Jordan: It's very wet in here.

Stomach: Indeed. Those are the digestive fluids. They help to break up the food into small pieces.

Jordan: I'll never look at Morgan the same way again!

Stomach: Normally, you'd be in here for a few hours. But since this is a special trip, we'll speed things along.

Jordan: Thanks.

Pickle: The food has to get even smaller once it leaves the stomach. On to the intestines!

Small Intestine: *(in a high voice)* Hi there! I heard we had a visitor. Welcome to Morgan's intestines!

Jordan: You said intestines, with an "s" at the end. But you're just one big tube, right?

Small Intestine: That's right. We're like a big pile of garden hose. But we have two parts.

Jordan: The small intestine and the large intestine.

Small Intestine: Excellent! You'll meet my partner, the Large Intestine, in a little while. But first, a great big hug!

Jordan: Not again! I feel like I'm with my Aunt Hazel. She's a real hugger.

Small Intestine: Fluids help me break down the food even more. Your friend Pickle will get so small, you will hardly be able to see him!

Pickle: This is when some of the food goes into Morgan's blood, where it travels to the rest of his body to feed it.

Jordan: And the rest of the food?

Pickle: The rest goes to the large intestine. That's where the rest of me is heading now. Morgan doesn't need some parts of me. Those parts won't be digested. They will come out when Morgan goes to the bathroom. And now it's time for us to say good-bye.

Jordan: You mean I won't go to the large intestine? That's a relief!

Large Intestine: *(in a low voice)* Good to see you, Pickle! Come on down!

Pickle: I'll be right there, Large Intestine!

Jordan: Well, thank you, Pickle. It sure was an adventure. I learned a lot!

Pickle: My pleasure.

Jordan: So how do I get out of here?

Pickle: Repeat the magic words: *Hickledy, pickledy pig. Let me out and make me big!*

Jordan: *Hickledy, pickledy pig. Let me out and make me big.* Hey! It worked!

Morgan: Huh? What worked?

Jordan: Oh, nothing.

Morgan: I don't feel well. Maybe it was something I ate.

Jordan: That sounds about right.

Morgan: I'm going to go lie down. You can have my other pickle.

Jordan: Thanks. Hmmm, a pickle? I think I'll have a carrot stick instead!

The End